For Parker, my favorite reading buddy.
A special thank you to Mrs. Hardy, my 3rd grade teacher at Romona School.
You're the reason I'm a teacher and an author. —L. D.

To my parents, who taught me that reading
is one of the most important things in life. —V. T.

STERLING CHILDREN'S BOOKS
New York

An Imprint of Sterling Publishing Co., Inc.
1166 Avenue of the Americas
New York, NY 10036

STERLING CHILDREN'S BOOKS and the distinctive Sterling Children's Books logo
are registered trademarks of Sterling Publishing Co., Inc.

ISBN 978-1-4549-2572-9

Distributed in Canada by Sterling Publishing Co., Inc.
c/o Canadian Manda Group, 664 Annette Street
Toronto, Ontario M6S 2C8, Canada
Distributed in the United Kingdom by GMC Distribution Services
Castle Place, 166 High Street, Lewes, East Sussex BN7 1XU, England
Distributed in Australia by NewSouth Books
Univeristy of New South Wales, Sydney, NSW 2052, Australia

For information about custom editions, special sales, and premium and corporate purchases,
please contact Sterling Special Sales at 800-805-5489 or specialsales@sterlingpublishing.com.

Manufactured in China

Lot #:
2 4 6 8 10 9 7 5 3 1
12/18

sterlingpublishing.com

Design by Heather Kelly
The artwork for this book was created digitally and with watercolor.

JUST READ!

BY

Lori Degman

ILLUSTRATED BY

Victoria Tentler-Krylov

STERLING CHILDREN'S BOOKS
New York

HOORAY!
I know how to read on my own!

But sometimes I don't want to do it alone.
So . . .

I read with an astronaut,
pirate, or farmer.

I read with a clown or
a knight wearing armor.

I read with a penguin,
a moose, or a bear.

I read . . . with . . . a . . . t o r t o i s e . . . or read with a hare.

Sometimes it's hard to know what things to choose.
So I just start reading—I've nothing to lose!

I read secret messages written in code.

I read funny signs on
the side of the road.

I read things that scare
me or cause me to grin.

I read about places where
I've never been.

Sometimes I can't seem to find enough time.
I steal a few minutes—it isn't a crime!

I read while I'm waiting to hear my name called.
I read while we're driving and traffic has stalled.

I read after raking the leaves into piles.

I read while I stroll down the vegetable aisles.

Sometimes it's boring to read just one way.
It gets so monotonous day after day!

I read while I'm spinning or
sliding or swinging.

I read when I'm drumming
or strumming or singing.

I read with my fingers
across bumpy lines.

I read with my voice or
my hands, using signs.

Sometimes it seems like there's no place to go.
So I start exploring and go with the flow.

I read in a bus, on a train or a plane.
I read in a cave or outside in the rain.

I read in a tree or below in its shade.
I read while I march in my hometown parade.
Sometimes I don't know the who, where, or when,
but that doesn't stop me . . .